Stillwater and Koo
SAVE THE WORLD

BY JON J MUTH

SCHOLASTIC PRESS · NEW YORK

For Molly

Remember to turn on the moon.

Koo stretched fuzzy toes and paws and yawned.

"Good morning," said Stillwater.

"Good morning, Uncle.
Warm and sweet smells woke me up.
Is it breakfast time?" asked Koo.

"Yes!" said Stillwater.
"What would you like to do?"

"Something important!
Fix all the things that are wrong.
Let us save the world!" said Koo,
taking a bite of waffle.

"That's a very big idea," said Stillwater.

"Breakfast was so good.
Waffles are my favorite.
Let us get to work," said Koo.

"Okay," said Stillwater.
"Maybe we can begin by tidying your room."

"When I put my things
where they go, I feel happy.
Not so jumbled up," said Koo.

"Jasper came to help.
He likes to sleep in the sun.
He might be hungry!" said Koo.

Stillwater said, "Let's feed him, and maybe change his litter box. Jasper might like to be brushed, too.

When we are finished, we can visit the fish pond."

"I wonder, do fish
swim knowing how very big
the vast ocean is?" asked Koo.

"That's a wonderful question," Stillwater said. "Let's think about it. Meanwhile, we can clear the leaves and feed the fish."

"Let us be certain
no one goes to sleep hungry
in the whole wide world," said Koo.

"Shall we make a welcome
gift for our new neighbors?"
asked Stillwater.

"Thank you for the cake!" said the Sanams.
"We feel so welcome in our new neighborhood,"
Mrs. Sanam said.

Stillwater and Koo wished them a good day and
hoped they would see them again soon.

"The Sanam family loved
your cake!" said Stillwater.

"Making a good cake
that you want to be just right
is not so easy," said Koo.

On their bike ride, Koo told Stillwater,
"I woke from a dream.
I'm worried about the world.
How can we fix it?"

"These are big feelings.
Let's stop here for a moment," said Stillwater.

"The world is so big.
But in my dream it wasn't.
It was delicate," Koo said.

"The world *is* delicate. It is our home, and it takes care of us.
We must always, every day, make our best effort
to take care of the world *and* each other," said Stillwater.

"Uncle! There's a truck!
A mama and baby ducks!
Look! Up on the road!" Koo pointed.

Koo was right! Stillwater saw a mother duck and her ducklings about to cross the road. A truck was coming, and the duck family was in danger!

Stillwater ran toward the road.
Koo was right behind.

With arms wide, like a crossing guard, Koo escorted
the baby ducklings to the other side of the road.

"I don't believe fish
know how big the ocean is.
They just do their best," said Koo.

"Yes," said Stillwater.

"Is saving the world
even possible at all?
I am still not sure," said Koo.

Stillwater smiled. "My bighearted Koo. You did so many things today that made the world a better place!"

"Each time you do something good, you save the world a little bit," said Stillwater. "And you will do a little bit more tomorrow."

Author's Note

The woes and burdens of the adult world don't exist separately from the world of children. The challenges children face every day are many.

Children want very much to make the world better, and they look to adults for guidance. A warm smile, holding the door for the person behind you, the kindness of sharing what we have with others — all of these acts are simple but profound. Raising our children to value spontaneous kindness gives them enormous and immediate power, because the smallest acts of kindness may save the world.

— Jon J Muth

Thousands of candles
can be lit from a single candle
and the life of that single candle
will not be shortened or diminished.
— A Buddhist teaching

Everything is perfect,
but there is a lot of room for improvement.
— Shunryu Suzuki

SCHOLASTIC PRESS

Library of Congress Cataloging-in-Publication Data is available.
LC Number: 2021045659

10 9 8 7 6 5 4 3 2 1   23 24 25 26 27
Printed in China   38
First edition, February 2023

Jon J Muth's drawings were created in watercolor and pencil.
The type was set in Fournier. The book was printed and bound at RR Donnelley Asia. Production was overseen by Jaime Chan. Manufacturing was supervised by Irene Chan. The book was art directed by David Saylor, designed by Charles Kreloff, and edited by Dianne Hess.